I Can Brown Skin

Andréa Galvin

Triple Treasures Publishing—Madison, WI
ISBN: 979-8-21853876-7
Library of Congress Control Number: 2024922588
Title: *I Can Brown Skin*
Author: Andréa Galvin
Paperback | 2024

Published in the United States by New Book Authors Publishing

Dedication

To my brown skinned lovies, AG4,

You inspire me daily to live with joy, laugh with abandon, and love without limits. Your patience, understanding, and unconditional love are the foundations upon which this work is built. Thank you for being the light in my life. This is for you.

I can count to infinity.
I can tie my shoe.
I can draw the whole world.

And I can fly to the moon.

I can, brown skin.

I can own the runway.

I can own my own business too.

I can dance to any song.

And I can hula hoop.

I can, brown skin.

I can sing from the heart.
I can make music move.

I can do my own hair.

And I can bake like Mama too.

I can, brown skin.

I can write what I feel.

I can talk about it through and through.
I can be sad from time to time.

And I can be happy too.

I can, brown skin.

I can help with the dishes.

I can take out the trash.
I can vacuum, sweep, and mop.

And I can run my own bath.

I can, brown skin.

I can travel the world.
I can see all there is to see.

I can fly like the birds.

And I can move like the sea.

I can, brown skin.

I can smile big smiles.

I can give big hugs.

I can say please and thank yous.
And I can share lots of love.

I can, brown skin.

I can, brown skin.
You can, brown skin.

Do all the things that we wish,
Brown skin.

I can, brown skin.

About the Author

Andréa Galvin is a new and upcoming author, who has developed a very empowering voice through her creative writing and her loving heart. She's a Louisiana native, raised in Madison, WI, city girl with a country heart. Andréa prides herself on being an educator, a mother of three, a mentor to the youth and those around her, and a lifetime learner. Andréa desires to connect with the youth through her writing, while inspiring them to be any and everything they want to be.